To Isobel and Alasdair – 16 and 18. How did that happen? I feel old!
J.A.

First American edition published in 2012 by Boxer Books Limited.

First published in Great Britain in 2012 by Boxer Books Limited
www.boxerbooks.com

Text and illustrations copyright © 2012 Jonathan Allen

The illustrations were prepared digitally by the author.
The text is set in Adobe Garamond Regular.
ISBN 978-1-907967-20-7

1 3 5 7 9 10 8 6 4 2

Printed in China

All of our papers are sourced from managed forests and renewable resources.

Don't Copy Me!

Jonathan Allen

Boxer Books

"What a great day for a walk
in the fresh air,"
said Little Puffin to himself,
taking a deep breath
and striding out.

But he had company.
Small Gull, Tiny Gull, and Baby Gull
were secretly following him
and copying everything he did.

Little Puffin noticed them
out of the corner of his eye.

How annoying!
Little Puffin turned around suddenly.
"Are you following me?"
he said, thinking he'd scare
the Gull chicks away.

"Are you following me?"
copied Small Gull.

"Are you following me?"
echoed Tiny Gull.

"Follow a me?"
said Baby Gull,
pretending there
was someone behind him.

The Gull chicks weren't at all scared.
They seemed to be having a great time.
Little Puffin tried again.
"Go away, and stop copying me!"
he shouted.

"Go away, and stop
copying me!"
copied Small Gull.

"Go away, and stop
copying me!"
echoed Tiny Gull.

"G'way . . . Stop copy me!"
laughed Baby Gull.
This was a great game!

Little Puffin didn't think so.
He thought it was a rotten game.
But how was he going to make it
stop? Little Puffin thought hard.

Small Gull, Tiny Gull and
Baby Gull copied him.
How annoying!

Suddenly, Little Puffin took off at a run.
"This will lose them!" he said to himself.
"They'll never keep up with me!"

But Small Gull, Tiny Gull and Baby Gull
kept up with him easily.
And what's more, they copied the way he ran.

How annoying!

Little Puffin stopped.
"Look, this isn't funny!" he said.

"Look, this isn't funny!"
copied Small Gull.

"Look, this isn't funny!" echoed Tiny Gull.
"Look . . . Funny!" said Baby Gull.

Poor Little Puffin.
The Gull chicks' silly game
almost had him beaten.

Then he had another idea.
If he sat very, very still, the Gull chicks
would have nothing to copy.
Then they'd get bored and go away.

So Little Puffin sat very, very still.

Small Gull, Tiny Gull, and Baby Gull
sat very, very still too.

Little Puffin sat and sat.
Small Gull, Tiny Gull,
and Baby Gull sat and sat.
But Tiny Gull and Baby Gull
started to fidget.
"Aha!" thought Little Puffin.

"This is b-o-o-ring!" said Tiny Gull eventually.
"Bo-o-o-o-rin!" said Baby Gull.

"You're right," said Small Gull.
"Come on, let's go and do
something else!"
So Small Gull, Tiny Gull,
and Baby Gull wandered off.

"Hooray!" said Little Puffin,
when he was sure they were gone.
"I knew it would work!
I'm just too smart for
those silly little Gulls!"

"Now, what was I doing? Ah, yes.
I was going for a nice, quiet walk —
by myself!"

"What a great day
for a walk in the fresh air!"
said Little Puffin to himself,
taking a deep breath
and striding out.

But he had company. . . .